This book belongs to

....

for
absent
friends
X —T. H.

Henry Holt and Company, LLC
Publishers since 1866
175 Fifth Avenue
New York, New York 10010
mackids.com

Henry Holt® is a registered trademark of Henry Holt and Company, LLC.
WINTER WONDERLAND
Words by Dick Smith / Music by Felix Bernard
© 1934 (Renewed) WB Music Corp.
All Rights Reserved
Used by Permission of ALFRED MUSIC
Illustrations copyright © 2016 by Tim Hopgood
This edition published by arrangement with Oxford University Press.
All rights reserved.

Library of Congress Cataloging-in-Publication Data is available.
ISBN 978-1-62779-304-9

Our books may be purchased in bulk for promotional, educational, or business use. Please contact your local
bookseller or the Macmillan Corporate and Premium Sales Department at (800) 221-7945 ext. 5442
or by e-mail at MacmillanSpecialMarkets@macmillan.com.

First published in 2016 by Oxford University Press
First American edition—2016
Printed in China by Leo Paper Group,
Gulao Town, Heshan, Guangdong Province

1 3 5 7 9 10 8 6 4 2

The drawings in this book were created using pencil, calligraphy ink, wax crayon, and chalk pastel.
They were collaged and colored using QuarkXPress and Adobe Photoshop.

Walking in a WINTER WONDERLAND

BASED ON THE SONG BY FELIX BERNARD AND RICHARD B. SMITH

AS SUNG BY
Peggy Lee

ILLUSTRATED BY
tim hopgood

HENRY HOLT AND COMPANY
NEW YORK

Sleigh bells ring,

are you listening?

In the lane, snow is glistening.
A beautiful sight, we're **happy** tonight . . .

Walking in a
WINTER
WONDERLAND.

Gone away is the bluebird.

Here to stay
is a new bird.

He's singing a song, as we go along · · ·

Walking in a

WINTER
WONDERLAND.

In the meadow, we can build a snowman.
And pretend that he's a Santa clown.

We'll have lots of fun with Mister Snowman.
Till the other kiddies knock him down.

When it snows,
ain't it thrilling?

Though your nose
gets a **chilling**.

We'll frolic and play

the Eskimo way···

Walking in a
WINTER WONDERLAND

In the meadow, we can build a snowman.
And pretend that he's a Santa clown.

We'll have lots of **fun** with Mister Snowman.
Till the other kiddies knock him down.

Later on we'll conspire, as we dream by the fire,
To face unafraid the plans that we've made . . .

Walking in a **WINTER WONDERLAND.**

Walking and we were talking . . .

While we were walking in a

Winter Wonderland
Sung by Peggy Lee

By Felix Bernard and
Richard B. Smith

Sleigh bells ring, are you listening?
In the lane, snow is glistening.
A beautiful sight, we're happy tonight.
Walking in a Winter Wonderland.

Gone away is the bluebird.
Here to stay is a new bird.
He's singing a song, as we go along.
Walking in a Winter Wonderland.

In the meadow, we can build a snowman.
And pretend that he's a Santa clown.
We'll have lots of fun with Mister Snowman.
Till the other kiddies knock him down.

When it snows, ain't it thrilling?
Though your nose gets a chilling.
We'll frolic and play the Eskimo way.
Walking in a Winter Wonderland.

In the meadow, we can build a snowman.
And pretend that he's a Santa clown.
We'll have lots of fun with Mister Snowman.
Till the other kiddies knock him down.

Later on we'll conspire, as we dream by the fire,
To face unafraid the plans that we've made.
Walking in a Winter Wonderland.
Walking and we were talking . . .
While we were walking in a Winter Wonderland.

"Winter Wonderland"

is one of my favorite songs, and one that's played over and over again in our house throughout the winter months. Peggy Lee's jazzy, upbeat version is particularly charming, and hearing it conjures up happy memories of winter walks in the woods with my family and friends.

No matter how old you are, I think the wonder and excitement of waking up to a world under a blanket of snow still remains, because as the song says, there's nothing quite as thrilling as a snowfall! And that's what this book is all about: the joy of being outside on a beautiful snowy day.